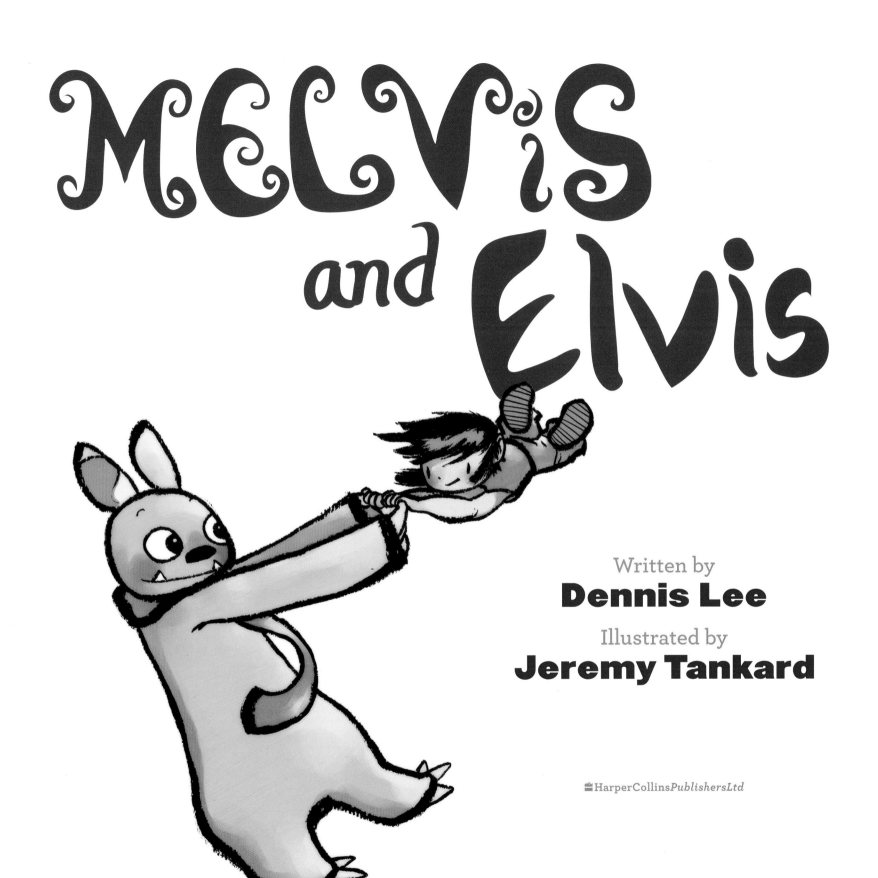

MELVIS and Elvis

Written by
Dennis Lee

Illustrated by
Jeremy Tankard

HarperCollins*Publishers*Ltd

For Sacha
D.L.

For Hermione and Theo;
and also for the kids at Queen Victoria Annex
J.T.

Melvis and Elvis
Text copyright © 2015 by Dennis Lee.
Illustrations copyright © 2015 by Jeremy Tankard.
All rights reserved.

Published by HarperCollins Publishers Ltd in 2015.

First edition

HarperCollins books may be purchased for educational, business
or sales promotional use through our Special Markets Department.

HarperCollins Publishers Ltd
2 Bloor Street East, 20th Floor
Toronto, Ontario, Canada M4W 1A8

www.harpercollins.ca

"Dancing Snowmen" and "In Cabbagetown" were written for the
Lost Songs of Toronto cabaret at Soulpepper Theatre Company.
The melodies were by John Millard.

No part of this book may be used or reproduced in any manner
whatsoever without the prior written permission of the publisher,
except in the case of brief quotations embodied in reviews.

Library and Archives Canada Cataloguing in Publication information
is available upon request.

ISBN 978-1-44341-148-6

Printed and bound in United States of America.
PC 10 9 8 7 6 5 4 3

CONTENTS

MELVIS AND ELVIS

Melvis the monster
And Elvis the elf
Were hunting for books
On the library shelf —

One on the carpet,
And one in a chair,
So neither one knew
That the other was there.

Now, Elvis was hoping
To pick out a story
With pictures of monsters
Both friendly and scary,

While Melvis was learning
To read by herself,
And she thought, "What I need
Is the tale of an elf."

Well they sought and they searched
And they searched and they sought,
They pulled down the books
And they thumbed through the lot,

But hard as they hunted,
And search as they might,
Nothing they looked at
Was totally right.

Then Elvis said, "Phooey!"
And Melvis said, "Bother!"
And with that, they spun round
And they stared at each other.

Said El, "You're a monster."
Said Mel, "You're an elf."
Then they shouted *"Hurray!"*
And they banged on the shelf —

For each was astonished
At what they could see:
A storybook person,
As real as could be.

Then Elvis taught Melvis
To play hide-and-seek,
And they raced round the room
Till their bladders were weak,

Hiding in secret
(For real or pretend),
And whooping it up
When they found their new friend —

Till at last it was time
For a quieter game,
And Melvis taught Elvis
To spell his own name.

Then Melvis helped Elvis
Reach high on the shelves,
And he pulled down a book about
Monsters and elves,

And tucked in a corner,
Like bears in a den,
They read it, and read it,
And read it again.

Open this book,
And you will see
A secret path
Called POETRY.

Follow the path,
And you will find
A home for your heart,
And a treat for your mind.

SLOPPY JOE

Sloppy Joe was slurping up
His slurpy, sloppy soup.

Sloppy Joe went crazy, with a
Holler and a whoop.

A beetlebug was swimming
In the gumbo, round and round.

Sloppy Joe cried, "Tally ho!"
And slurped the beetle down.

MONKEYDOODLES

Three little monkeydoodles, climbing up a tree,
Stealing drops of honey from a big fat bee.

One met a caterpillar, one made a fuss,
And one rode to heaven on the Bloor Street bus.

4

I WISH I WAS

I wish I was a fireman.
I'd wear a great big hat.
I'd rescue people with my hose,
And then I'd save the cat.

MISTER KIM AND HIS WONDERFUL CAT

Mister Kim, at the corner store,
Taught his cat to sweep the floor.

Soon the cat could stock a shelf,
And fill the cooler by herself,

Count the money, brew the tea,
And cash the tickets for the lottery.

She ran that store both night and day
(While Mister Kim chased the mice away).

WHEN I WOKE UP

When I woke up on Monday,
I found I was a pony;
I felt so fine at breakfast time
I ate some macaroni.

When I woke up on Tuesday,
I found I was a goose;
I felt so fine at breakfast time
I drank some apple juice.

When I woke up on Wednesday,
I found I was a fly;
I felt so fine at breakfast time
I ate a pumpkin pie.

When I woke up on Thursday,
I found I was a whale;
I felt so fine at breakfast time
I drank some ginger ale.

When I woke up on Friday,
I found I was an eel;
I felt so fine at breakfast time
I ate an orange peel.

When I woke up on Saturday,
I found I was a trout;
I felt so fine at breakfast time
I ate a Brussels sprout.

When I woke up on Sunday,
I found I was a snake;
I felt so fine at breakfast time
I ate a birthday cake.

THE TALE OF THE TERRIBLE TOOTHPASTE

I sort of squoze the toothpaste
And it splatted on the floor,

So then I tried to put it back
The way it was before.

But every time I squished it in,
It squiggled out some more —

So that is why I hid it
In the bottom of the drawer.

DAVY

Davy, Davy
    Joined the navy,
Brushed his teeth
    With meat and gravy,

Sailed his ship
    Across the sea,
Said, "This is
    The life for me."

TO A BULLY

We don't like measles,
And we don't like flu.
We don't like bullies,
And we CAN'T STAND YOU.

WISHBONE

A wishbone, a squishbone,
A double-dirty dishbone,
Your mother caught you on a hook
And that's why you're a fishbone.

MARY McGREGOR McGUFFIN McGEE

Mary McGregor
McGuffin McGee
Went for a ride
On the TTC.

She rode on the subway
To Paris, France,
And she danced all day
In her purple pants.

She rode on the subway
To Santa Cruz,
And she danced all night
In her dancing shoes.

The trip was amazing!
And when it was done,
She said, "My adventures
Have just begun."

And with that she rode home
On the TTC —
Mary McGregor
McGuffin McGee.

CALLING ALL DINOSAURS

Calling all dinosaurs —
Come to the Museum.
Triceratops has disappeared, and
Nobody can see him.

Stegosaurus, hurry!
Brontosaurus too!
Triceratops is missing, and we
Don't know what to do.

12

He might have gone to Russia,
He might have gone to Rome,
He might have gone to Calgary
To find his dino-home,

Or else he got in trouble, and
We have to run and free him.
Calling all dinosaurs —
Come to the Museum!

DANCING SNOWMEN

Snow, snow,
Everywhere you go,
The snowmen dance
In Ontario.

Hey, hey,
They dance all day —
Till the sun comes out
And they melt away.

SLEEPING WITH BEARS

In olden days,
When I was three,
I took my bears
To bed with me;

But now I am big,
And the bears are too,
And they stay on the shelf
Like big bears do —

Except if they're lonely,
Late at night,
And they might need a kid
To hold them tight,

Or else they're scared
('Cause you know that a bear
Can still get scared
When there's nothing there);

So we whisper together
And then we agree —
Tonight, they can sleep
In the bed with me.

IS YOUR NOSE TOO SMALL?

Is your nose too small?
Can you find your nose at all?
Does it hide behind the door
When the neighbours come to call?
Does it vanish when you grab it
Like a disappearing rabbit?
Is your nose —

        too —

             small?

Are your feet too big?
Do they wooffle like a pig?
Do they march around the town
While your legs are lying down?
Could they fill a Spanish villa
Like an overweight gorilla?
Are your feet —

        too —

             big?

Is your brain too hot?
Does it catch on fire a lot?
Does your mind begin to sizzle
When you think a little thought?
Could you fry a corn tortilla
When you get a bright idea?
Is your brain —

        too —

             hot?

HOPELESS

You're totally hopeless!
        You scratch at the door,
You chew on the sofa,
        And pee on the floor.
You whimper all night,
        And you scamper all day,
And when I get angry
        You want me to play.

Then you stare up at me
        With your big goopy eyes,
And you waggle your tail
        Like a furry surprise,
And I'm ready to scream —
        So I pet you, and then
We're totally, hopelessly
        Friends again.

DANGEROUS DAN

Dangerous Dan
        Was a bad, bad man —
He wouldn't eat his porridge.
        So they put him away
        For a year and a day,
In a place called Criminal Storage.

        But Dan had a plan,
        And a friend called Stan,
And Stan had a truck named Lola.
        So they drove to the Coast,
        Where they gobbled down toast
And mountains of crunchy granola.

SACHA'S PUCK

Sacha put his hockey puck
Inside his jacket pocket.
He hung it in the locker, but
He clean forgot to lock it.

A picky-pocket person came
And stole the puck away.
What rotten luck! Without a puck,
How can poor Sacha play?

IF I WAS A MONSTER

If I was a monster,
    I'd live on my own.
I'd live in my home, and be
    All alone.

Alone, so alone,
    I would live on my own,
And I'd dream about meeting —
    An elf!

19

THE TREE

Beside the Severn
   Stands the tree
That bore the branch
   That sheltered me —
That gave me my
   Enchanted place,
And made my heart
   An ache in space.

BOBOLINK

Bobolink, bobolink,
    Take me along.
I'll be the silence
    And you be the song.

I'll be the meadow
    And you be the tune.
Bobolink, bobolink,
    Fly away soon.

IN CABBAGETOWN

In Cabbagetown there lived a dog
And I don't know why, but he loved eggnog.
He drank all day and he got real fat —
Till his belly exploded, and that was that.
    Imagine that!
    The dog got fat —
    His belly exploded
    And that was that.
    Imagine that!
    He got real fat
    Till his belly exploded
    And that was that.

In Cabbagetown there lived a cat
And I don't know why, but she acted like a brat.
She picked her teeth with a ping-pong bat —
Till her teeth exploded, and that was that.
    Imagine that!
    The cat was a brat
    The dog kept drinking
    Till his belly got fat.
    Yes the cat was a brat
    And the dog got fat —
    Till they both exploded
    And that was that.

In Cabbagetown there lived a giraffe
And I don't know why, but he loved to laugh.
He cackled like a loon in a laundromat —
Till his head exploded, and that was that.
    Imagine that!
    He laughed and laughed
    The cat was a brat
    And the dog got fat —
    Till they all exploded
    And that was that.
    Yes that — was — that!

In Cabbagetown there lived a rhinoceros
And I don't know why, but he looked like
    Frankensteinoceros.
His nose was horny and his feet were flat —
Till the horn exploded, and that was that.
    Imagine that!
    His feet were flat
    The giraffe just laughed
    And the cat was a brat,
    Yes the cat was a brat
    And the dog got fat —
    Till they all exploded
    And that was that.

In Cabbagetown, there lives a man
And I don't know why, but he likes to play the ban- (jo).
The creatures all gathered by the chair where he sat,
Till he put them in a song — and this is that.
    Imagine that!
    The song says that
    The rhino's feet were flat
    And the long-neck laughed;
    The cat was a brat
    And the dog got fat —
    Till they all exploded
    In a song that was loaded
    With a laugh that ho-ho-ho-ded
    Till it nearly overfloweded —
    And this — is — this — is — *that*!

    (*SPLAT!*)

IF I WAS AN ELF

If I was an elf,
    I'd live by myself;
I'd live by myself
    On a cool elf shelf.

On my cool elf shelf
    I would live by myself,
And I'd dream about meeting —
    A monster!

STRAWBERRY WISHES

Strawberry wishes
    And blueberry dreams,
Come and we'll wander
    By rivers and streams.

Sugarbush snowy
    And buttercups warm,
We'll go together
    Through sun and through storm.

STINKARAMA

Doodle, doodle, poppyseed strudel,
I've got a friend and he smells like a poodle.

Smells so bad it rots your nose —
Killed a skunk and a bunch of crows.

Smells so bad it fries your brain —
Drove a grizzly bear insane.

Push him down a wishing well —
Still can't stop that awful smell.

Hang him up on the CN Tower —
Still can't kill that *ee-yew* power.

Stinkarama, stinkaroo,
What's a poor boy gonna do?

Stinkarama, stinkaree,
Take that friend away from me.

APOLOGIES TO MY MOST NOBLE AND EXCELLENT FRIEND

I'm sorry that I squished your nose;
I thought it was a garden hose.

And I'm sorry that I squashed your belly;
I thought it was a sack of jelly.

It wasn't nice to rip your shirt off
(I only meant to get the dirt off).

And it wasn't kind to fry your socks
(Besides, they tasted hard as rocks).

How awfully rude to break your knee —
I don't know what came over me;

And pounding on your head all night
Was fun. But *very* impolite.

THE NOTAPOTAMUS

I thought I saw a potamus,
Asleep upon a cotamus,
But when I reached the spotamus,
The potamus was notamus.

It must have got monotamus,
Just sleeping on that cotamus —
So, feeling hot-to-trotamus,
It took off like a shotamus!

O naughty notapotamus,
I liked your style alotamus.
In story, song, and thoughtamus
You're gone, but not forgotamus.

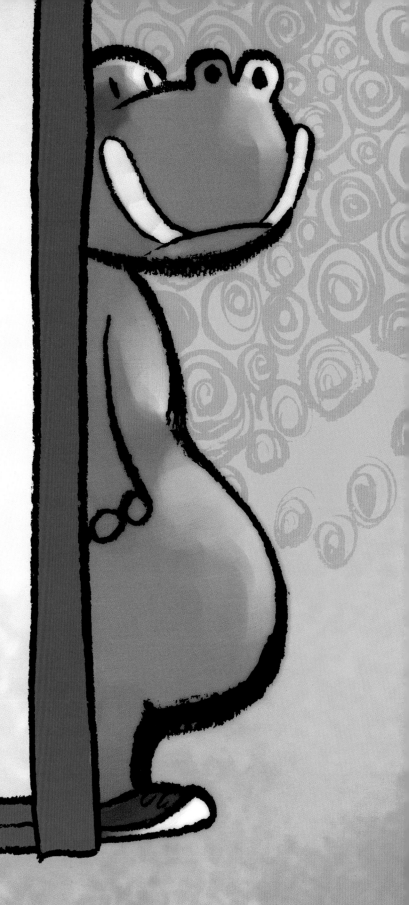

THE NEW FRIEND

If you could like me,
  Like me now,
As deep as the dreams
  In your heart allow.

I don't know why,
  And I don't know how —
But if you could like me,
  Like me now.

THE SUN GOES DOWN

The sun goes down in Coboconk,
In Killaloe and Wawa,
And we go down to sleepy town
In Perth and Petawawa —

Like birds that flutter to the nest
In Mono and Elora,
Or drowsy deer near Capreol,
Or Minto, or Kenora.

THE WIZARD

I went to see the wizard
In the middle of the night.
His eyes were fierce and far away,
His cloak was burning bright.

"O wizard, can you teach me
How to rise and fly away?"
He stared at me, and glared at me,
And taught me what to say:

　　"Zoomberry, zoomberry, zoomberry pie:
　　Zoomberry, zoomberry, now I can fly."

I said it once, I said it twice,
I said it three times three;
With mighty shout I bawled it out
Until he growled at me,

"You have to say it softly,
You have to say it slow,
You have to whisper it at night
As off to sleep you go:

　　"Zoomberry, zoomberry, zoomberry pie:
　　Zoomberry, zoomberry, now I can fly."

So home I went, and down I lay,
And closed my sleepy eyes,
And as I whispered "Zoomberry,"
I felt my body rise.

Then up I floated, off I flew,
The whole wide world to see —
And now each night I tell the spell
The wizard taught to me:

"Zoomberry, zoomberry, zoomberry pie:
Zoomberry, zoomberry, now I can fly . . ."
(Zoomberry, zoomberry, now I can fly.)

A SONG FOR MISTER LEE

A flea can fly,
A fly can flee,
And now, a song
For Mister Lee:

Dum-dee, dum-dee,
Dippity doo,
Ferry me over
The ocean blue —

Dum-dee, dum-dee,
Dippity dye,
Float me away on a
Dragonfly —

34

Dum-dee, dum-dee,
Dippity din,
Whisk me along on a
Fish's fin —

Dum-dee, dum-dee,
Dippity dee,
Trundle me home on a
Circus flea.

A flea can fly,
A fly can flee,
And now, goodbye
To Mister Lee.

ONE BOOK HEAVY

One book heavy,
One book light,
One book waiting
For an elf tonight.

One book cozy,
One book wild,
One book waiting
For a monster child.

One book funny,
One book true,
One book waiting
For a kid — called — YOU.